MW01491159

THEATER

BOY SCOUTS OF AMERICA
IRVING, TEXAS

Requirements

1. See or read three full-length plays. These can be from the stage, movies, television, or video. Write a review of each. Comment on the story, acting, and staging.

2. Write a one-act play. It must take 8 minutes or more to put on. It must have a main character, conflict, and a climax.

3. Do THREE of the following:

    a. Act a major part in a full-length play; or, act a part in three one-act plays.

    b. Direct a play. Cast, rehearse, and stage it. The play must be at least 10 minutes long.

    c. Design the set for a play. Make a model of it.

    d. Design the costumes for five characters in one play set in a time before 1900.

    e. Show skill in stage makeup. Make up yourself or a friend as an old man, a clown, an extraterrestrial, or a monster as directed.

    f. Help with the building of scenery for one full-length play or two one-act plays.

    g. Design the lighting for a play; or, under guidance, handle the lighting for a play.

4. Mime or pantomime any ONE of the following chosen by you and your counselor.

    a. You have come into a large room. It is full of pictures, furniture, and other things of interest.

    b. As you are getting on a bus, your books fall into a puddle. By the time you pick them up, the bus has driven off.

   c. You have failed a school test. You are talking with your teacher. He does not buy your story.

   d. You are at camp with a new Scout. You try to help him pass a cooking test. He learns very slowly.

   e. You are at a banquet. The meat is good. You don't like the vegetable. The dessert is ice cream.

5. Explain the following: proscenium arch, central or arena staging, spotlight, floodlight, flies, center stage, stage right, stage left, stage crew, stage brace, batten.

6. Do two short entertainment features that you could present either alone or with others for a troop meeting or campfire.

33328A
ISBN 0-8395-3328-4
©1999 Boy Scouts of America
2001 Printing of the 1999 Edition

Contents

A scene from *Neville's Island* by Tim Firth. *Stage West Productions; photo by Buddy Myers.*

Curtain Going Up!

Everybody loves a show. We feel a little thrill of excitement as we wait for the curtain to go up on a stage play, or for a movie or television drama to begin. Will it be funny? Will it be sad? Will the story grip us so that we are not just watching but are almost a part of it?

Sometimes, of course, we are disappointed. Maybe the story does not seem real. Maybe the actors seem like actors, not real people. Maybe the lines that are supposed to be funny aren't funny at all. So we feel let down.

But the next time we're waiting for a drama to start, we'll still experience that same thrill. Everybody loves a show.

Now a much greater thrill awaits you. To earn the Theater merit badge, you will go behind the footlights to see the view from the other side. You will learn how a drama is put together by studying three plays and by writing one yourself. You may take part in a play, either as actor, director, or one of the backstage workers, and you will try your hand at creative dramatics by showing your counselor that you can communicate feelings and emotions through pantomime or mime.

Your first step in earning the Theater merit badge is to talk it over with your counselor. He or she will guide you as you begin studying plays and writing one, and as you choose among the options in requirement 3.

A scene from *Greetings!* by Tom Dudzick. *Stage West Productions; photo by Buddy Myers.*

Thinking Critically

Many newspapers and television and radio stations employ a person called a *critic*. The critic's job is to describe a play or movie and tell about its strong and weak points so the readers or listeners will have an idea whether they want to see it.

For requirement 1, you'll look at plays as a critic would. You will find that thinking critically about a play will teach you a great deal about the theater. You will begin to notice how a play is put together. If you are watching a performance, you will see how actors produce the effects that make an audience laugh or cry. You'll see how scenery can help a play— or perhaps how some dramas can be more effective with almost no scenery. You will notice how the actors are placed in certain positions so that the stage has balance, and how the audience's attention is held by the character who is the focus of interest at each moment.

You may also form ideas about how the production could be better. Perhaps you will feel, as you watch with a critical eye, that one of the actors is not as good as he might be in the part. Or perhaps the setting may look false to you. Maybe you'll find that you can't really believe in the story or the characters. In brief, you will be looking at the play with the eyes of a critic.

There are no hard-and-fast rules for drama criticism. We all see a play for ourselves. We bring to it our own knowledge of how people behave, our own attitudes toward life, and perhaps prior knowledge of the play itself. In a way, we can say that each spectator sees a different play because of what he or she brings to the theater.

Therefore, your opinions of a play might be quite different from the opinions of others. But the critic's opinions are more valuable than most because a critic is expected to know more about drama and acting than do most people.

How to Do It

The first part of requirement 1 calls for you to either read three plays or see three full-length productions. Or, you can read one or two plays and see one or two others.

There are advantages in reading plays and other advantages in seeing them. If you read a play, you are more likely to notice strengths and weaknesses in the story than if you only see the play performed. On the other hand, because plays are written to be performed rather than read, you are more likely to see the full possibilities of the play if you see it performed. Either way, your job for this requirement is to look at plays and perform the role of a theater critic.

Suppose you are going to meet the requirement by seeing three plays. For each one, take your notebook to the theater or sit down with it in front of your TV set. Concentrate on the drama. Let yourself be entertained, but at the same time have questions like these in mind.

- Do you believe in the story? Of course, in a play about ghosts or a fantasy like *Peter Pan,* you don't really believe. But if the story is good, you will be able to *suspend your disbelief.* That is, you'll be persuaded to set aside your doubts if a ghost story or a fantasy is so good as to make you believe that it *could* happen that way—as if there really were ghosts or if people could fly.

- Do the actors seem like real people? Or do they seem like— well, like actors?

- Are the *sets* or backgrounds right for the play? Or do they seem out of place?

- Does the play make you *feel* emotions? Love? Hate? Joy? Sympathy? Grief? Or does it leave you cold?

- How could the play be better? Would a different twist to the plot make it stronger? Would the play be more dramatic if one of the characters were different?—an old man instead of a young one, for example? Or a weak man instead of a brave one? Is the setting right? Would the play be more appropriate in a midwestern town than in New York?

- Are the costumes right for the play? And the lighting? Is the actor who should be the center of interest kept there at all times?

Ask yourself these questions as you watch. Other questions will occur to you, too, if you keep alert.

The same types of questions will apply if you are reading a play instead of seeing one. Of course, if you are reading a play, you can't comment about such things as the directing, the stage sets, costumes, or lighting, but you can still look at the story with a critical eye.

Soon after you have finished reading or seeing a play, write down your ideas about the plot and how successful the play was. Were all the loose ends tied up? Were all of the false leads explained? Does the *foreshadowing* (the "hints" or clues about what's to come) become clear? Don't wait. Write down your impressions while they are fresh.

To complete requirement 1, you do not have to write a long review the way a newspaper drama critic would. Each review can be about a page long. If you see a great many things to write about, you may want to make your reviews longer, but there is no need for you to try to analyze each production as thoroughly as a professional critic would.

A scene from *Fences* by August Wilson. *Stage West Productions; photo by Buddy Myers*.

A scene from *Peter Pan,* Haltom High School Theatre Arts presentation

Live Theater

If you are fulfilling this requirement by seeing rather than reading, try to see stage plays if possible. The reason a stage play is better than a movie or television drama for this requirement is simple: The movie or TV director can focus your attention on a very small part of the action, cutting out anything that does not matter at that moment. But the stage director must make the audience look at the part that matters and forget everything else that's on the stage at that moment. This makes the stage director's job a little harder. Therefore, you are likely to learn more about the problems of drama from a play with live actors than from a movie or a TV drama.

You should be able to find live theater near your home, at least occasionally if not regularly. Perhaps your own school sometimes has a play. Many towns have a community theater that presents several plays a year.

TV and Video

If you decide to meet this requirement by watching TV dramas, choose dramatic shows that last at least an hour and a half. Most of the shorter programs are much the same, week after week. The dialogue changes, of course, and the plots are slightly different, but the characterizations don't change much. The viewer can be pretty sure that the hero will win the girl or the fight, or that he will blunder through somehow.

Instead of series television, bring your fresh critical eye to a production that tries for real drama and vivid characterization such as might be found in PBS's *Masterpiece Theater* presentations. You can also find a number of plays at your video store such as Kenneth Branagh's *Hamlet* or *Othello,* or plays by Horton Foote.

A video is excellent for critical evaluation because you can rewind and see the same scene again to give you time to take in all the details. Also, seeing the same scene done by Mel Gibson as Hamlet and Kenneth Branagh as Hamlet can give you a number of ideas about directors' choices and interpretations of a play.

Playwright William Shakespeare (1564–1616)

Writing a Play

The purpose of requirement 2 isn't to make you a skilled *playwright*, capable of writing a play that Broadway theatergoers can't wait to see. That would be asking too much of you.

Good playwrights have a natural creative urge that has been perfected through years of hard work and practice. Not everyone has the dramatic instinct, and not everyone can write dialogue that sounds natural on the stage. The playwright must have both of these qualities, which are rather rare.

But that doesn't mean you should not try to write for the stage. You might find that you do have a flair for writing plays. Whether you do or not, you will learn a great deal about the difficulties of playwriting and about the theater itself by trying to write a drama.

There are many books on writing plays, going all the way back to Aristotle, a philosopher from ancient Greece. Most of the books are loaded with terms like *exposition, crisis, empathy, premise, complication, climax,* and *thesis.* These words have meaning for experienced playwrights and the writers of books—although sometimes the same words can mean different things to different writers.

These books also offer rules for writing plays, almost as if the playwright's art can be reduced to a formula. The rules, however, have been broken or amended by playwrights from Shakespeare to David Mamet and Neil Simon. In another form of theater called the Theater of the Absurd, the rules are broken more often than they are observed.

As a beginning dramatist, you will do well to avoid becoming wrapped up in unfamiliar words and slippery theories about how plays are written. Your job is to try to find a single dramatic idea and then make that idea live on stage by surrounding it with characters drawn from life.

Decide on an Idea

Where do you get an idea for a play? Mary Higgins Clark, a novelist, says she likes to look at ordinary situations, then ask herself, "What if . . . ," and fill the blank with possible actions. However, no one can give you a sense of what is dramatic and what is not. If you get an idea that you think might be good for a play but you're not sure, ask your merit badge counselor or your English or drama teacher about it. Chances are, they will be able to tell you whether your idea can be developed into a drama.

In the simple drama you are trying to write, the most important thing is to have some sort of *conflict*. This conflict might be between the wills of two people, a person against a natural force such as a flood or tornado, or a person struggling with some aspect of society such as dress codes or divorce. Reduced to its simplest terms, your plot might be described as "Boy meets girl, boy loses girl, boy wins girl." Of course, there might not be a girl in it at all. The point is that there will be some sort of conflict in your play, and the conflict will be resolved somehow.

Find a Character

One good way to find a plot for your play is to think about people you know. Often you can develop a plot by starting with a particular person you know well who has an outstanding character trait.

For example, perhaps you know a Scout who is such a good example of the Scout Law that it might almost have been written to describe him. You could take this Scout and place him in a situation where his character is tested. You might make him the son of an impoverished family who has a chance to get a great deal of money by doing one tiny dishonest act that no one will ever know about except himself.

There you have the seed of a drama. The Scout would be the main character. The conflict would be the Scout's struggle against wrongdoing. And the climax of the play would be the point at which he makes his decision.

Maybe there is a boy in your troop who is rather clumsy and awkward, but everyone likes him because he is honest

Neil Simon
Courtesy Bill Evans & Associates

and straightforward. And there is another Scout who is a good athlete, quick to learn, but vain. Everyone jokes with the awkward boy, but it's all in fun except for the good athlete. He is a bully and constantly makes fun of the other boy. At camp, a Tenderfoot who cannot swim falls into the lake, and these two Scouts are the only ones nearby. Which one fishes him out and which one runs away in a panic? That is drama, too. The main character would be the awkward Scout, the conflict would be the opposition of the two characters, and the climax would be what happens when the untrained Tenderfoot almost drowns.

August Wilson
Courtesy Dena Levitin

Write your play about things you know. Don't take a chance on a subject or setting about which you know little. If you do, both the story and the characters are likely to sound false. You will not make your audience believe in the story or the characters if *you* don't believe in them.

Make a Scenario

Don't plunge into writing dialogue the minute you have decided on your dramatic idea, your characters, and your plot. Instead, make an outline of your play, from the opening words, through the *climax* or big scene, to your final dialogue. This is called a *scenario*.

A scenario is an important step in writing a play because, if you do not have your drama well planned, you are likely to find yourself rewriting and rewriting. Even though your play will have only one act and one set, you will need a scenario to keep you on track from start to finish. As you write, you may decide to make changes in your scenario, but at least it will keep you from wandering off into dialogue that does not advance the plot.

As you make your scenario, you must keep in mind your setting—what it looks like and where each of your characters will be at any moment. Prepare a short biography of each of the most important characters, too, to help you bring them to life. It is not enough for you to know that Jim is a Scout. You should know whether Jim is tall, short, fat, or thin, how old he is, and whether he lives by the Scout Law. Such facts about your characters may never enter your drama, but if you have each character fixed in your mind as a living person, it will be easier to bring your drama to life.

Write Dialogue

Have you ever listened closely to a group of friends just chatting on some subject? If you haven't, try it. You will be surprised how disjointed it seems when you pay close attention to each sentence. The conversation is likely to be full of "wells" and "uhs" and "you knows." There may be sentences within sentences. And yet, somehow all the sentences finally come together in a meaning everybody can understand.

The challenge in writing dialogue for the stage is cutting out all the unnecessary phrases—everything that is not vital to the story or the characterization—and at the same time maintaining the flavor of natural speech. If you are writing a dialogue between two Scouts, they must sound like Scouts—not like college professors or small boys. At the same time, you must compress their speech. If you wrote down exactly what two Scouts might actually say, you would have so many words that it might be long past the audience's bedtime before you got to the climax of your play.

Here are a few things to remember when writing dialogue:

• Make it easy to say. Avoid tongue-twisting words, and keep sentences short.

• Read it aloud. If a Scout is speaking, does his part sound like a Scout, or does it sound like the speech of a senator or an announcer in a television commercial?

• Does the dialogue move your story along? Don't insert a joke in the dialogue unless it advances your plot or tells the audience something about one of your characters. You might like the joke, but it will distract the audience unless it's part of the story.

Trim the Excess

A one-act play written by a professional dramatist would probably run about 10,000 words—about as much as a very long short story. As a beginner, you won't want to aim that high. A play of perhaps 10 or 12 handwritten pages (eight to 10 typewritten or computer-printed, double-spaced pages) should be about right for your first effort. This length will give you enough room to develop one dramatic idea and resolve it. You won't have much room for embellishments or for a deep exploration of the characters of the people in your play. (Of course, if your play turns out to be longer than 12 pages, that's fine.)

Study This Sample Play

Now take a look at a concrete example to see how to write your scenario and begin your play. Let's suppose that your patrol leader has left the troop to go into Venturing. The assistant patrol leader seems to be a natural to take over as patrol leader. He is a First Class Scout, he seems to have leadership ability, he learns skills quickly and easily, and the other boys like him well enough. Sometimes he's careless, though, and he is not always kind and patient with some of the younger Scouts who do not catch on to things as quickly as he does.

Also in your patrol is another First Class Scout who is quiet and reserved and who learns more slowly but thoroughly. He does not seem to be a natural leader, although he goes out of his way to help the Tenderfoot Scouts.

Now let's put these two boys into a situation where their leadership qualities will be tested. Before writing a scenario, let's first write short biographies of these two Scouts so that we have their characteristics firmly in mind. About like this . . . .

Matt—The assistant patrol leader of the Beaver Patrol, he firmly expects to be elected patrol leader. In fact, he cannot imagine not being elected. Matt is a First Class Scout, tall, handsome, athletic. He is vain about his ability. He doesn't boast a lot, but he fishes for compliments from the younger Scouts. Matt is nearly 14 years old and has stopped advancing; he feels satisfied as a First Class Scout.

Ryan—A First Class Scout, 13 years old, he has earned three merit badges and is working on others, trying to reach Star rank soon. He is quiet and reserved, but friendly to all. Ryan is of average height and build, not especially athletic. The other Scouts like him, but no one seems to have thought of him as a possible patrol leader. He takes the time to help the Tenderfoot Scouts with their advancement work and never makes fun of them when they are slow or awkward. Ryan would like to be patrol leader but has never given it serious thought; he assumes that Matt will be chosen.

Now you have the main characters in mind. The conflict will be between these two, and the climax will be the situation in which their leadership is tested. Let's put the Beaver Patrol on a hike during which there is an emergency—a brushfire, for example. Which Scout will react as a leader should?

The Scenario

Here's the scenario.

- The scene is a clearing in the woods where the Beaver Patrol has stopped for lunch. It is autumn. The woods are dry, and the leaves and brush crackle underfoot as the Scouts hike.

- As the play opens, two Scouts are talking about their former patrol leader, wishing he were along. Their discussion informs the audience that the patrol is to elect a new leader the following week and that Matt is the obvious choice. Neither of the two Scouts seems very enthusiastic about picking Matt.

- As acting patrol leader, Matt directs the building of a fire for the patrol's lunch. He tells the Scouts not to bother cleaning the fire area except for the foot or two where the fire will be.

- Ryan advises Matt to tell the Scouts to clean loose debris from a 10-foot-wide circle around the fire spot. Matt laughs at him and calls him a neat freak.

- The other Scouts are a little uneasy about Matt's carelessness but are won over by his charm.

- While the patrol is cooking hot dogs, an ember spits from the fire and lands in nearby brush, smoldering slightly. Matt quickly puts it out. Ryan again points out that it would be safer to clear everything that could burn from a wide circle around the fire. Again Matt laughs at him.

- The patrol eats lunch. Afterward, Matt organizes a game. He tells the Scouts to leave the fire and let it burn itself out.

- Ryan says he will douse the fire first, but Matt orders him to join the game. Reluctantly, Ryan leaves the fire.

- As the game goes on, Ryan casts an occasional glance at the fire. Suddenly he sees that it has spread into the brush and is beginning to blaze furiously.

- He calls to Matt and the other Scouts. Matt gathers up his pack and calls for the other boys to get out of there with him.

- Ryan directs them to stay and put out the fire. They do, with Matt hanging back and watching.

- As the play ends, the same two Scouts who were talking when it began are in conversation again. It is clear from their discussion that they will choose Ryan as their new patrol leader. In the background, we hear Matt blustering that the fire was not serious, and, anyway, he could have put it out all by himself if he had thought it was necessary. Ryan says nothing. As he starts for home, the patrol falls in behind him, with Matt, still talking, bringing up the rear.

That's the scenario for the play. It is nothing but a skeleton that will need a good deal of fleshing out, but it gives an outline to follow in writing the dialogue.

The Script

The opening dialogue of this little drama appears on pages 22–23, to show you the format your finished script should follow. This is not the whole play, but just enough to give you the idea.

Notice the stage directions, underlined and enclosed in parentheses. As you prepare your own finished script, you will want to add occasional stage directions and advice for the actors on how a line should be said. Don't overdo this. The director will be in charge of bringing your play to life on the stage. Leave most of the directing to the director.

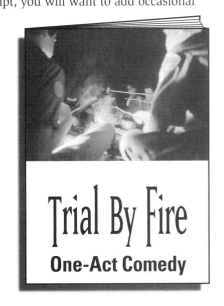

Trial By Fire
One-Act Comedy

TRIAL BY FIRE

A Comedy in One Act by John Scout

<u>Characters:</u>

MATT—assistant patrol leader, Beaver Patrol

RYAN—a First Class Scout

STEVE—Scout

ADAM—Scout

JEFF—Scout

ERIC—Scout

PETE—Scout

<u>Scene:</u> A clearing in the woods. At left, the audience sees MATT standing over two Scouts who are building a fire. RYAN watches. STEVE and ADAM are at right, gathering twigs and fallen branches for the fire. Behind MATT we see dry leaves and undergrowth. A line of trees surrounds the clearing. As the curtain opens, STEVE and ADAM, apparently some distance away from the others, are talking as they gather wood.

STEVE: You know, Adam, this hike doesn't seem like much fun with Dave gone.

ADAM: Yeah. He was a cool patrol leader. I mean, Dave really knew how to run things so everybody had a good time. He knew his stuff, too!

STEVE: He sure did! Remember that time we were up by the West Branch and Eric fell in the creek? That was before he could swim, and—

ADAM: Dave got him out of there almost before we knew he'd fallen in. He knew his stuff all right. But if I were Dave, I'd want to be in Venturing, too. I can see why he'd want to leave us.

STEVE: Me, too. Say, Adam, how d'ya think Matt will do if we elect him patrol leader?

ADAM (doubtfully): OK, I guess.

STEVE (thoughtfully): I don't know. He looks like the right guy, but still . . .

ADAM: Well, he's been assistant now for three or four months, so he ought to know something about it.

STEVE: Yeah, I guess so.

ADAM (stirring the leaves with his foot): Boy, these leaves are really dry!

STEVE (picking up a twig and breaking it): Look at that! It's like a matchstick. These woods will go up in smoke if we have a fire before we get some rain. Well, let's haul this wood back.
(They gather their wood and move toward the fire site. JEFF and ERIC are making a tepee fire lay. PETE is handing them twigs. MATT and RYAN are standing over them.)

RYAN: I still say, Matt, you ought to have them clear out a bigger space before they light the fire.

MATT (scornfully): What's with you, Ryan? You being a neat freak again?

JEFF (uncertainly): Maybe we should do like Ryan says.

MATT (sharply): Never mind, Tenderfoot! Do it like I tell you. I say you've cleared out all you need to, so just leave it like that! Stop whining.

JEFF: OK, Matt, whatever.

(JEFF and ERIC prepare to light the fire.)

* * *

Writing Your Own Play

When you have your characters and setting in mind and have completed your scenario, start writing your own play. Here are a few simple things to keep in mind, not as rules but as guides, as you write.

• Early in the play, let the audience know the characters and what the problem is.

    In "Trial by Fire," all the characters are Scouts, and the audience can tell this because the boys are in uniform. It's established right away that Matt is the assistant patrol leader and that he is the logical candidate for patrol leader. It's also clear, to a Scout audience at least, that Ryan knows his Scouting; having him caution Matt about the way the fire is being built shows Ryan's competency. It also suggests a conflict between the two Scouts.

- Plant some hints early in the play that will make your big scene or climax more effective.

    The climax of "Trial by Fire" is to be a brushfire that causes Matt and Ryan to show their true colors. The dialogue between Adam and Steve strongly hints at the danger of fire.

- Try to increase the suspense as you build up to the climax.

    In the "Trial by Fire" scenario, there's a scene in which an ember spits from the fire and starts smoldering in brush while the Scouts are cooking. This builds up the suspense, foreshadowing the bigger fire. In the script, another conversation between two Scouts could be inserted about who should be elected patrol leader. This would reinforce the question in the audience's mind that was planted during the talk between Adam and Steve as the first scene of the play opened.

- Put the climax near the end of the play.

    An audience wants to know how a drama comes out. Once you have shown that, it will be hard to hold the audience's interest much longer. In "Trial by Fire," the climax is the brushfire and Ryan's leadership in putting it out while Matt hangs back. As soon as that is over, a short conversation between Adam and Steve, in which it is made clear that they will elect Ryan as their patrol leader, ties up the plot. Ryan leading the patrol as the Scouts start for home emphasizes the point. Then the curtain comes down.

Acting a Part

You probably played make-believe all the time when you were younger. Maybe you still do, although now you may be making believe in your mind only. If so, it means your creative imagination is still at work, and it could be a sign that you will make a good actor.

If you can possibly do requirement 3a, do it! In no other way can you get quite the same thrill of working in the theater as by acting a role in a play. You can learn a great deal about the theater by doing other jobs such as directing or designing, but if you are acting, then you are at the heart of the theater.

Maybe there is a drama club or class in your school that puts on plays now and then. If so, join it and try to win a part. Or maybe there's a community or children's theater in your town. That would offer excellent opportunities for you, not only to get acting experience but also to learn about every facet of the theater.

If these opportunities are not open to you, how about your troop? Are there three or four other Scouts who would like to try their hand in the theater? If so, perhaps you could get together and plan a play for your next troop outing. It might not be Broadway quality, but it will be fun for you and the troop. At the same time, you will learn much more about the theater by taking part in an actual production than you would by reading all the books on drama in the library.

Qualities of an Actor

What qualities do you need as an actor? To begin, you need a voice that can be heard distinctly at the back of an auditorium. You also need a good memory because you must be able to remember hundreds of lines and bits of stage directions. A good memory is mainly a case of being able to focus or concentrate, and such concentration can be learned.

You also need self-assurance—the confidence that you are capable of the part you're playing and the conviction that you can convince the audience to believe in your character. Self-assurance comes with practice.

You need a good imagination. Without imagination, your character won't come alive. Ninety-nine percent of acting is imagination.

With these qualities, all of which can be acquired, you can be a good actor. The greatest actors have an additional quality that is difficult to describe. It is a force of personality that energizes the audience as if a spark of electricity were passing back and forth between actor and spectators. Alec Baldwin has it. So do Danny Glover, Glenn Close, Anthony Hopkins, Whoopi Goldberg, and Mel Gibson. Not everyone can be a Baldwin or a Glover. But by working hard and studying, you can become a fine actor.

Danny Glover
Courtesy Rogers & Cowan

Auditioning for a Role

When you *audition* or read for a part, don't waste valuable energy worrying about whether your auditioners will like you. Get up there and show them your work. If your audition starts out shaky, don't be afraid to stop and ask to begin again. It would be foolish of you not to change direction.

Occasionally, after a good reading, the director will ask you to read again and offer you an acting adjustment. Many times, that's really done to see if you can take direction; it might not have anything to do with the scene or your own interpretation. Other times, the director may be looking for different qualities in your persona or personality.

Portraying a Character

Once you have the part, the first and most important approach for the actor is to read the play and find out what the playwright wants to say to the world. *Who, what, where,* and *when* are some of the questions you should ask yourself when you first get a part.

- **Who Am I?** What kind of person is this character I'm to play? As your character, you must know how old you are. What grade are you in, or have you already finished school? As your character, you must decide what your favorite color is, what your favorite food is, what food you detest, what your favorite TV shows are, the type of music you like or dislike, etc. In short, you must know the same things about a character that you know about yourself.

- **What Time Is It?** When does the action take place? What kind of a day is it? *Example:* "It's 7:00 A.M. on Saturday morning and I am (as your character) getting ready for a campout. It's cloudy with a light rain falling."

- **Where Am I?** Where does the action take place? *Example:* "I am in my bedroom and it is a mess, so I have to spend time digging in the closet for my equipment. I can hear the sound of music coming from the stereo in my brother's room, which is down the hall."

- **What Surrounds Me?** What objects are around me? *Example:* "My backpack is on the floor along with my camping gear, rain gear, clothes, swim trunks, and toothbrush."

- **What Are the Given Circumstances?** What is the situation? What events are taking place? *Example:* "My family has just moved here, so this is a new troop for me. John, from three doors down, and his dad will pick me up in 20 minutes, and I'm not ready."

- **What Do I Want?** What are my objectives? *Example:* "I want the other guys to like me. I want to make friends. I want to do a good job so others will respect me."

- **What Is in My Way?** What obstacles confront me? *Example:* "I'm nervous and a little scared because I don't know anyone. I can't remember everything I need. I can't find all my gear."

- **What Must I Do to Get What I Want?** What actions do I take? *Example:* "I make a list of everything I will need and check it off as I find things. I mentally make a list of funny stories so I will have something to tell around the campfire. I will volunteer to help teach others a skill I already know such as how to pitch a tent or pack a backpack."

Another important part of portraying a character is to know yourself. You must know who *you* are, as well as who your character is. You must find your own sense of identity, enlarge this sense, and learn to see how that knowledge can be put to use in the characters you will portray on stage. Many directors will tell you that when you audition, it isn't just the reading that gets the actor the role. It's the actor's qualities, plus the reading, that does.

Remember, therefore, that your own identity and self-knowledge are the main sources for any character you may play. Director Lee Strasberg said, "If we cannot see the possibility of greatness, how can we dream it?" And Sanford Meisner, a noted New York acting teacher, reminds us that acting is living truthfully under imaginary circumstances.

Handling Stage Fright

After you have addressed the audition and thought through your character, your next question might be, "What if I get stage fright?"

You may indeed experience this feeling. But you won't be alone. Many great actors have struggled with stage fright. You will find, just as they have, that the rewards of acting soon banish this fright. If you can dispel your fear and act in a play, do it. There is no other comparable thrill.

Directing a Play

An author has written a play, a producer has decided to stage it, and now its fate is in the hands of a director. The director will be in complete charge of the production. What the audience finally sees will be what the director has achieved.

Probably most of the plays you will take part in will be produced and directed by an adult—perhaps a teacher in your school or the director of a community theater. So if you are going to direct a play for requirement 3, you may have to organize your own players from among your friends and fellow Scouts. Perhaps you could stage the final performance at a troop meeting.

You might want to present your own play, which you wrote for requirement 2. If that does not seem suitable, read a few of the plays listed in the back of this pamphlet. Almost certainly you will find one there that interests you and falls within your ability to direct.

Visualizing

Your first step as a director is to study the play you have chosen. A director must read and reread the play to get a full understanding of what the author is driving at, what sort of people the characters are, and the setting for the play. Before casting or planning any other details of production, the director must "see" the play completely in his or her mind.

The author will not have filled in every detail about each character. The author probably did not indicate the physical appearance of each person, and may have left gaps in revealing their personalities. Fill these in with your imagination, based on your knowledge of the script.

If you study a script carefully, you may find yourself imagining one person as noble but vain, tall and handsome, and a little neater in his dress than the average guy. You might see another character as a blunderer, slight in build and nervous, and careless in his clothes and grooming. Develop these images in your mind as you think about a particular play.

Casting

All of this study will be a big help to you when you begin casting the play. If your conception of the play's hero is a tall, dark-haired, handsome man, don't give that part to your best friend who is short, stocky, and blond—especially if he's a poor actor. Try to fit the actor to the play character, rather than making the character fit the actor. This may take some tact and diplomacy, particularly if your best friend thinks of himself as a pretty talented actor. But you must choose the right person for each part, or you will find your production drooping even before the dress rehearsal.

How should you go about making your choices? There are several methods. Of course, if you have seen all the candidates perform before, you already know how well they can act. But suppose you don't know them that well. You might ask each one to read a short scene from the play. This will give you an idea of how well they express themselves and their ability to project an emotion or a thought.

Another good way to find out who can act best is to let each of the candidates read through the play. Then ask each one to perform a scene—not word for word, of course—by improvising and making up lines. These improvisations will help you choose the best actor for each part.

Once you have made your choices for the cast, stick to them unless it is absolutely necessary to change. Most people will not be offended if they are not picked for the best part, but almost anyone would be hurt if he were removed from his part without a very good reason.

Rehearsing the Play

Cast members should be prepared by practicing their lines even before the first rehearsal. At the first rehearsal, you will want to have the actors read through their parts and begin to learn their lines. During the second rehearsal, talk to them about the movements you want them to make. You and each of the actors should have a script to work from, and even before the first rehearsal, you should have made some notes on your script.

Your notes ought to include what you want each actor to be doing and where he should be on the stage during each scene. You might want to make changes later, but you should have some ideas before rehearsals start.

When you have decided these things, your actors can make notes in their scripts about these movements. This process of planning the stage business is called *blocking*.

By your third or fourth rehearsal, the cast members should know their roles well enough to run through the play without scripts and without much prompting.

For the dress rehearsal, the actors are in costume and go through the entire play without stopping.

Your job now is to refine the performance until each actor seems to be getting the most out of his part and until the play moves briskly along to its climax.

The final preparation is called the dress rehearsal. Some productions—especially those that have elaborate costumes—may have more than one dress rehearsal. At a dress rehearsal, the actors, wearing their costumes, go through the entire play without interruption. In addition, all scenery and lighting effects are used.

Your Other Duties

While you are in the early stages of preparation—maybe even before you have chosen the cast—you, as the director, have some other things to worry about: the stage itself, the setting, the costumes, the props, and the lighting. Probably you will have to handle these duties yourself, unless you are lucky enough to be directing a fairly big production in your school or church.

These other duties are described later in this pamphlet, in the discussions of other options for fulfilling requirement 3.

Staging the Play

At the time of the performance, the director's job is over. Directors who have done their job well have nothing to do when the curtain rises—except watch the performance, of course.

Of course, in the small type of production you are likely to be directing, you may also be the lighting operator, the propman, a stagehand, and the prompter. If so, you will be among the busiest people in the theater.

Designing a Set

Commitment is very important to the design process because if you are not committed to doing your best work, your design will be inadequate. The first step in set design is to read the script. As the designer, it is your job to read through the script and evaluate all of the *entrances* and *exits* to create a thumbnail sketch. (An entrance can be through a door, a window, or a curtain. It could be simply an actor walking on stage. An exit can also be through a door or window, etc.)

You must determine the setting of the play. This will help you design a set that reflects the time and period in which the play is set. Examples might include Victorian, medieval, or perhaps primeval.

As the designer, you will need to decide if you want an *abstract set* or a detailed, extravagant set. (An abstract set is not realistic. For example, a ladder might represent a mountain or a tree. A fruit crate could be a rock, a chair, or a bush.) Beware of overloading the set. The audience comes to the theater prepared to use its imagination, so you don't have to show every tree and bush in the forest.

The style of architecture is also an important issue for set design. If the play is set in London, England, you would not want the architecture to be based on the high-rise buildings of New York City. If the characters in the play are from the poorest neighborhood of a large city, you would not want a design that looks like a middle-class suburb. Your design would be highly inaccurate. Sometimes it is a temptation for a set designer to create a beautiful picture on the stage without much regard for whether it fits the play. You must resist this temptation.

Another thing to take into account is the season and whether any holidays occur in the script. Keep in mind that each act might need a different type or style of set. You must also consider the mood of the play. This will help you determine the appropriate colors and textures.

As Shakespeare put it: "The play's the thing." The settings are only one part of the production. The set designer must bear in mind that settings are to be used by actors whose job it is to bring the play to life. The designer can help them to do that by effective sets, but the designer alone cannot bring the play to life.

A set design should provide an atmosphere in keeping with the play, and strengthen the illusion of reality. Nevertheless, it should not be so striking or fascinating that the audience gets lost in it and stops listening to the play.

Planning a Set

If you decide to fulfill requirement 3c by making a model of the set for the play you wrote for requirement 2, you won't have to study the script, of course. But you will have to think it over carefully to make sure that your set will enhance your play.

Your first question in planning the set is the stage itself. Is it very wide and shallow? Narrow and deep? Is it a proscenium (a stage framed by an arch), or an arena in which the audience surrounds the stage? Or is the play to be given outdoors at Scout camp? Clearly, the director and set designer cannot begin to plan settings until they have taken into consideration the limits of their stage.

At this point you should know the different elements the design calls for. Perhaps trees are needed, or tables, benches, a couch, or even a mountain. Perhaps the design needs a focal point around which the action of the play will revolve. In a famous mystery play called *Dial M for Murder*, the audience learns the answer to the question of "whodunit" through a door. In that case, this door will figure prominently in the design.

Using a ruler or architect's scale (see the *Model Design and Building* merit badge pamphlet) and these ideas, start an in-depth draft of your design. State which types of materials you think your set should be made of, such as wood, fabric, plastics, metals, or maybe plastic foam. Label the objects in your design. For example, if you have a door in your design, mark it "a 6-foot oak door with a 2-inch pine molding."

In making the set accurate, avoid doing too much or you will lessen the impact of the design. You must think of the *sight lines* from the audience's perspective—what the audience will be able to see on the stage. Therefore, you should have a ground plan, a front elevation, and the sight-line illustrations, which should be drawn to scale and in detail.

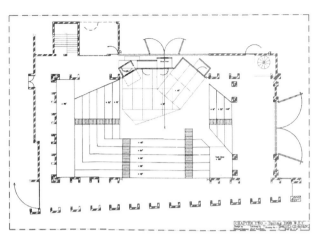

Ground plan

Front elevation

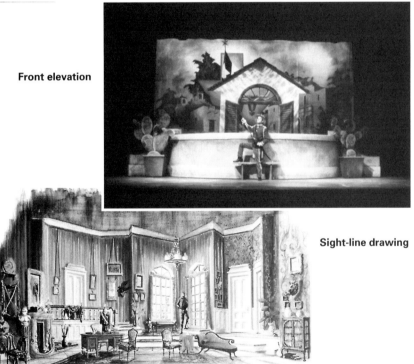

Sight-line drawing

A sight-line drawing uses a floor plan like the one you illustrated, and a floor plan of the auditorium. You find the farthest extents to which the audience can see and construct or plan the design around those limits. This not only helps in the construction of the set but also is a great help to the technical crew.

A front elevation design is done when you take the front view of a set and flatten it into a single plane. This will help people to see the height of the elements that your imagination has created. The ground plan is an aerial view or floor plan of the set indicating the width of objects used, so it must be very precise.

Building a Model

The final step is to create a model. The two types of models are the *functional model* and the *production model.*

A functional model is basically a thumbnail sketch put into three dimensions so that designers can see if their ideas work. A production model is complete in every detail. All of the *hand props* are included in a production model, which is the final product of a designer's imagination. (Hand props are things carried on stage or handled by the actors, such as canteens, letters, or glasses.)

A 3-foot-wide model is a good working size, but you can build your model set any size you want. For backdrops, use some gray cloth. Paint scenery on the cloth if the play calls for it, or simply hang the cloth as a neutral background. For props, you might use small toys and doll furniture, but remember to consider the character types. Are they collectors of odds and ends, or do they dislike clutter? These considerations determine the choice of props.

Once you have finished your ground plan, your front elevation, the sight-line drawing, and your model, you will have everything that you need to begin an accurate construction of your set. Designing a set takes hard work and requires a great deal of research and study to make a truly accurate set design, but the end result will be worth the effort.

For your first attempt at stage design for a single-set play, you can build a shoebox model. A "shoebox theater" is a suitable and inexpensive way to achieve a good visual of a set.

The backdrop can be made from a stiff piece of coathanger wire and a piece of paper. Use watercolors, crayons, or felt-tip markers to draw the scenery.

Cut the shoebox cover along the lines indicated in the sketch to make a valance or simulated curtain.

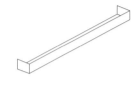

Cut the bottom and one side of the shoebox as shown. The rear opening will admit a light (a flashlight will do). The top opening will allow you to put in a backdrop.

Note the placement of the wires on the top of the shoebox. There should be room for two or three different backdrops.

Make small props such as trees and tents from the pieces of cardboard left over from the shoebox cover.

Designing Costumes

The costume designer enhances a play by dressing the actors appropriately, in much the same way that the set designer dresses the stage appropriately. The first step in costume designing is research. You must read the script and then study the time period in which the play takes place.

For requirement 3d, you are to design costumes for a play set in any period before the year 1900. Suppose you choose a play that is set in 16th-century England or 19th-century South Africa. Or your play is William Shakespeare's *Antony and Cleopatra*, set in ancient Rome. Or you choose a play with a pre-Columbian, Colonial, Revolutionary, or postbellum (after the Civil War) American setting. How do you find out how people dressed in those times and places?

Begin your research in your school or public library, where you can find costume and history books that show what people wore in different eras of history and parts of the world. Then, using your imagination, adapt the illustrations found in those books to the characters in your play. Don't just copy some drawings from a book. Add your own touches, while staying true to the period in which your play is set.

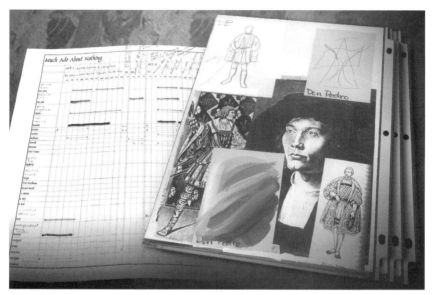

Working closely with the director helps a designer create costumes suited to the play and the era.

Design Sketches

After you have chosen the play and studied its period, you need to sketch your ideas. Preliminary sketching helps the costume designer in two ways.

• First, the sketches will be your initial means of visual communication with the director. From them, the director will be able to see what you want the costumes to look like.

• Second, and even more important to you, it is through the preliminary sketching process that most designers discover for themselves what the costumes will look like.

Color sample swatch
done in watercolor

Preliminary pencil sketches

Only rarely do costume designers conjure up complete, detailed costumes in the mind and then represent them on paper. The mind is more apt to visualize bits and pieces that reveal character types. You may have a notion, for example, that the sleeves should be long and flowing; you may know that the skirt must trail on the ground, but it's only when you have your pencil on the drawing paper that the individual images and notions come together into a design.

Costume design is like set design in that there is a great deal to discover about a script before you sit down to draw. But you should never put off sketching until you have everything in your mind in complete detail. That wait may well be in vain. The process of sketching is a process of designing. A sketch is not an illustration of a design; it is a design.

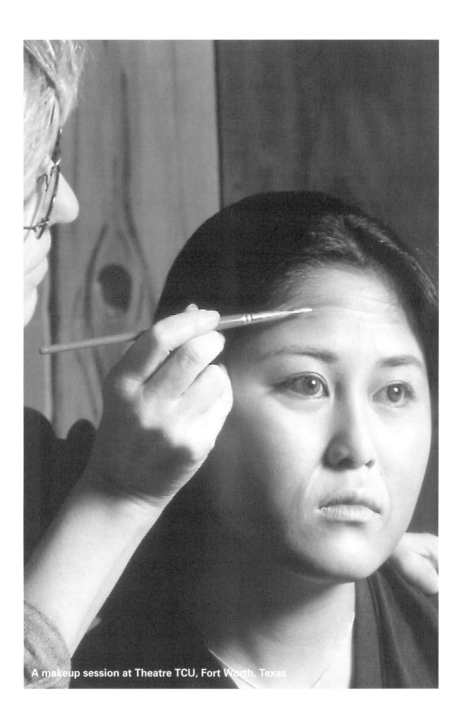

A makeup session at Theatre TCU, Fort Worth, Texas

Using Makeup

Remember when you were a small boy and you wanted to play pirates? You borrowed your mother's lipstick to draw jagged red scars on your cheeks and arms.

You will still find making up fun, but you ought to be much better at it now. For requirement 3e, you must be able to show your counselor real skill in applying makeup.

As you become skilled in using makeup, you will find it easy and fun to make up yourself or a friend as almost any character, from a clown to a bearded pirate to Abraham Lincoln. Try many characters. The requirement asks you to be ready to make up as one of four characters, but you will enjoy trying many other characterizations.

Purposes of Makeup

In the theater, makeup has several purposes.

- First, of course, it adds to the actor's characterization of his role. If he is playing an old man, he ought to look like an old man to the audience.

- Second, it is easier for the other actors to play their parts properly because they are reacting to an old man, not to Jim Smith, the guy down the street who goes to the same school they do.

- And finally, makeup helps the audience to see the actors clearly. The bright stage lighting tends to wash out an actor's face unless his features are emphasized by makeup.

For these reasons, makeup is very important to the theater.

Makeup Equipment

To do a proper job of makeup, you need a kit with several items. These can be fairly expensive, so borrow a kit if you can. Perhaps the school drama department or the community theater, if your community has one, will let you borrow a makeup kit if you replace the materials you use. Most of the materials can be bought at a discount store, but the total cost will be high if you must buy these yourself.

Here is what you need for a basic makeup kit.

- Cold cream or liquid makeup remover
- Foundation or greasepaint in assorted colors
- Creme and dry rouge in assorted colors, and a rouge brush
- Lipsticks in assorted colors
- Eye shadows and eye-shadow brushes
- Face powder in assorted colors
- Silk sponge, powder puff, and powder brush
- Eyeliners (blue, gray, and maroon) and eyeliner brush
- Nose putty
- Spirit gum and spirit gum remover
- Crepe hair in assorted colors (including your own hair color)
- Scissors, comb, and hand mirror
- Absorbent cotton and tissues

Using all this equipment requires much practice to achieve the effects you want. You would be wise to ask your counselor, or someone else who is experienced in the theater, for advice on making up.

Making Up

There is not enough room in this pamphlet to show you step by step the best ways to make up as an old man, a clown, an extraterrestrial, or a monster. But here are a few tips that may be useful as you practice.

- Your face should be absolutely clean before you begin applying makeup.

- Apply foundation or greasepaint first. It gives the proper color and base.

- However, to give a monster or an extra-terrestrial some grotesque bumps, use nose putty, which is soft plastic material that sticks best to dry skin. Put it on *before* applying foundation or greasepaint.

- To make a clown's rubber-ball nose, use a ball, cutting it to fit over your nose. Stick it in place with adhesive tape and spirit gum. Blend foundation or greasepaint to cover the edge.

- To make yourself look older, frown and wrinkle your forehead. With eye shadow, mark in the wrinkles. Make your lips and cheeks a little paler. Using eye shadow, darken the area under your eyes and put "lowlights" in your cheeks to make them look old and shrunken.

- To give yourself a bald head, use a tight-fitting bathing cap with slits cut for your ears.

- To put scars on a monster, draw them with dark lipstick or black liner and powder them.

To remove makeup, rub your face with cold cream or liquid makeup remover until the makeup is dissolved. Around your eyes, use only eye makeup remover—not petroleum jelly, baby oil, or anything other than eye makeup remover. (Using a product other than eye makeup remover could cause an infection around your eyes.) Then wipe your face with tissues until all the grease is off. Wash with soap and warm water.

With makeup you can go from Jim Smith to Frankenstein. All you need is practice, practice, and more practice!

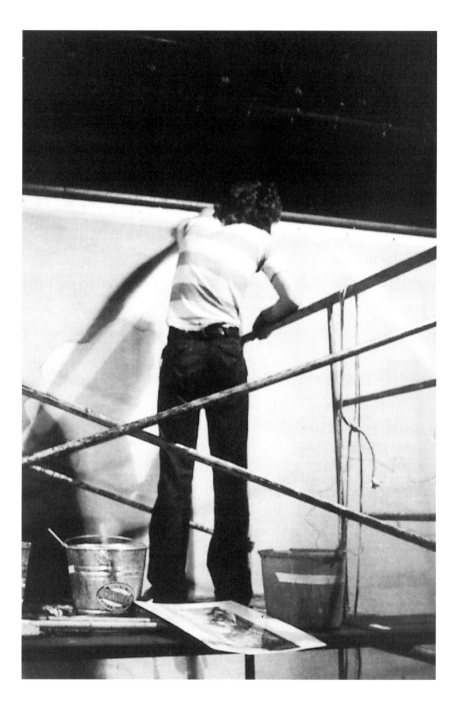

Building Scenery

The theater has a place for the artist as actor, director, or designer. There are many places for craftsmen, too—carpenters, electricians, painters, propmen. Requirement 3f calls for you to try your hand at a couple of these crafts. To fulfill the requirement, you will need to join a school drama group or community or children's theater in which you will have a chance to work on and actually build scenery.

Building Flats

There are many ways to achieve the effects called for by the set designer. Sometimes, for example, curtains of a neutral gray color provide much of the background for a play, with a few folding screens or flat shapes suggesting doors, windows, walls, or other special effects.

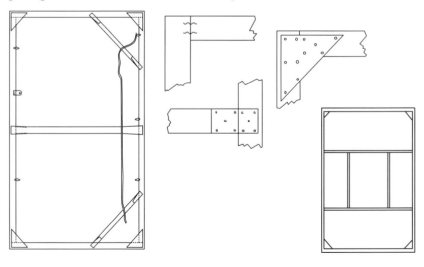

The flat on the left is plain and basic; the flat above is designed to include a window.

If you are building scenery for a play, you probably will be working mainly with *flats.* Flats are simply large frames with canvas or another material stretched over them. They are the basic unit of stage scenery. They are made of wood or steel tubing and are normally covered with muslin, plywood, or other fabrics and materials. Then they are painted as walls or windows or whatever is required for the play. Flats are light in weight so that they can be moved quickly and easily, and they can be used for different plays simply by repainting them a different color.

A standard wooden flat is 14 feet tall and 4 feet wide. Flats are usually made from straight white pine, 1" × 3" for the rails, stiles, and toggle bars. Although a flat can be assembled using mortise-and-tenon or halved joints for extra strength, most shops use butt joints when putting flats together.

You may help build some substantial flats if you are working in a school play. For a troop play, just use inexpensive folding screens or simple frames with cloth or canvas coverings.

A flat can be assembled using mortise-and-tenon or halved joints for extra strength, but most are put together with butt joints.

When stretching muslin over a frame, avoid stretching it tight; you need to allow room for fabric shrinkage when you paint the muslin.

Putting on the Canvas

For elaborate flats, use a piece of heavyweight muslin (128- or 140-thread count). The muslin should be slightly larger than the height and width of the flat. Stretch the muslin over the frame. Using a staple gun or tack hammer and tacks, attach the muslin along the inside edge of one of the stiles. Place the staples or tacks about one foot apart.

Move to the center of the other stile and pull the muslin until it barely sags across the face of the flat. Staple or tack it on the inside edge of the face of that stile. Be sure that you don't stretch the muslin until it is tight; you will need to allow room for fabric shrinkage when you paint the muslin.

Work your way toward the end of the flat, alternately pulling and stapling or tacking the material. Do this in both directions from the tack or staple that you placed in the center of the stile.

In a similar fashion, pull and tack the fabric to the inside edge of the face of both rails. If there are any wrinkles or puckers in the fabric, pull the staples or tacks and restretch the fabric until the wrinkles are removed.

To finish covering the flat, glue the muslin to the frame. Regardless of the shape of the flat, you should glue the covering only to the face of the rails and stiles. If the covering fabric is not glued to any internal pieces (toggle bars, corner braces), it will be able to shrink evenly when the flat has been painted. This uniform shrinkage will result in fewer wrinkles on the face of the finished flat.

To glue the cloth to the flat, turn back the flap of muslin around the edge of the flat and apply a light coating of glue to the face of the stiles and rails. Be sure that you use a thorough but light coating because if it soaks through the muslin, the glue may discolor or darken the paint job. Fold the muslin back onto the wood and carefully smooth out any wrinkles with your hand or a small block of wood.

After the glue has dried, trim the excess fabric from the flat. The easiest way to do this is to pull the fabric tight and then run a matte knife down the edge of the flat.

When this process is completed, you have a basic, multipurpose flat. There are many special types of flats for doors and windows that open, as well as such things as stairs and ramps, that you may need to make. Read about stage scenery in the books listed at the back of this pamphlet for some tips on building these.

Painting Scenery

Painting stage scenery is both an art and a craft. It's a good idea to have someone who is experienced in scene painting to work with you. One thing to remember as you begin painting is that the color will be lighter when it is dry than when it is wet. For that reason it is wise, before you begin painting, to test a little of the paint on a piece of paper or canvas to see how it will actually look.

A scene painter needs at least shades of yellow, brown, green, blue, red, black, and white in his workshop. The brushes used are

A scene painter strives not for realism, but for illusion. Keep it bold and simple.

ordinary housepainter's brushes. The 4-inch size is probably most useful, but brushes of all sizes will be necessary on many jobs.

The first step in painting a new flat is to prime it, just as you would if you were painting new wood. However, the main purpose of this priming is to tighten the canvas.

When the primer has dried, you can begin the real decorating. But give the job careful thought before you start slapping on the paint. If several of your flats are to be joined—to make a wall, for example—you must be sure that the paint is put on with that end result in mind. Otherwise, you might find that your painted moldings and wallpaper figures do not match up. Therefore, you must assemble the flats and mark each one in the order it will be used so you can be sure that the moldings or wallpaper figures will come together properly when the flats are joined.

The actual decorating depends on what your set design calls for. If you must mix paints to get the exact shade of a color you need, make sure you keep a sample of that exact color on a piece of paper or in a small can. This way you won't find your set having two different colored pieces that are supposed to be the same.

Keep your scene painting bold and simple. Remember that you are not striving for realism, but for an illusion. If you're not careful, small wallpaper figures will look blurred when viewed from a distance. Make everything as straightforward and as uncomplicated as possible.

Lights hung from pipes illuminate this thrust stage. *Stage West Productions; photo by Lee Angle Photography Inc.*

Lighting the Stage

Proper lighting techniques are important to any theatrical performance. Light is as important to the production as the actors or the script. The director and lighting operators, however, are limited in what they can do by what electrical equipment they have.

Stage lighting has six functions: visibility, mood, composition, focus, credibility, and unity. These six ideas must be applied and followed in every lighting job.

- **Visibility** is being able to see what is happening on the stage.

- **Mood** refers to the emotions stimulated by the light.

- **Composition** describes the picture created by the light.

- **Focus** is the ability of light to direct one's attention to a certain part of the stage.

- **Credibility** refers to the necessity of any light to be relevant to the dramatic situation.

- **Unity** is the ability of light to tie all other aspects of the show together.

Each of these functions of light plays a large role in every performance. Lighting operators achieve these functions by manipulating the *qualities of light*. The qualities are:

- **Intensity**—the quantity of light and shadow

- **Direction**—the angle at which the light hits the stage

- **Movement**—any change in light that suggests motion

- **Color**—used either in a realistic or highly artificial way; affects moods and attitudes and even perceptions of temperature

- **Texture**—a sense of planned variation in the pattern of lighting

There are two distinct but interrelated areas of stage lighting: the equipment that controls and distributes the electricity which creates the light, and the lighting effects that are created; that is, the design.

Stage Lighting Design

While a technical knowledge of equipment is important, a lighting designer must first be aware of the needs of the play to be lit. How best can the functions and qualities of stage lighting be manipulated for the production at hand?

The beginning designer should work to develop a sense of nature's own lighting effects in order to make informed, yet creative, decisions. Spend time examining how moonlight creates shadows and colors in the outdoors. Observe and try to count the number of colors in a sunset. How does the light of a campfire reflect off a lake onto the trees, and what mood does that create?

With each lighting design it becomes the designer's job to decide which colors, angles, and intensities of light best achieve the appropriate look for each moment of the play. Whether comic or dramatic, most plays take their audience on some sort of emotional journey. A "cool" stage (lit with blues, greens, and violets) will help establish calm feelings. A "warm" stage (lit with reds, ambers, and yellows) can intensify moments of excitement or anger. The angle of light can make a moment eerie (lit from the side), or produce striking silhouettes (lit from behind).

A designer must begin with a thorough knowledge of the play in production. Take notes in the script about the effects needed for each scene and the moods and feelings you think that creative lighting can help convey. Often a designer will sketch moments of the play requiring special attention.

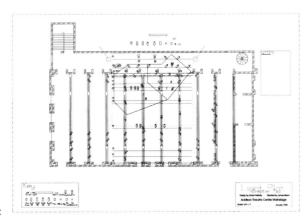

Lighting plot

From these sketches and notes, elements of design begin to take shape and the designer will start to draft the layout, or plot, for the design. It is in the drafting process that more complex technical decisions are made as to the exact type and location of each lighting instrument, electrical circuitry, color, and focus.

Lighting design, as with any creative task, is best learned through observation and experimentation. If you can't work with real stage lights, make your own instruments using coffee cans and porcelain lamp mountings. Change the color of the beam with colored plastic wrap or pieces of fabric. (Around hot lights, be careful not to burn yourself or the fabric or melt the plastic you're using for special effects.) Professional lighting gel can also be purchased affordably at almost any theatrical shop.

Lighting is among the most innovative of the theatrical arts. New instruments, colors, and techniques are constantly being developed. The design must always serve the entire production, but the ways in which that can be achieved are endless.

The Hardware

Light for the stage may be provided by an elaborate and extensive assortment of professional lighting instruments, miles of cable, and stacks of dimmers, all designed to meet the needs of the script and performance. However, few school stages are equipped for the kind of lighting effects that can be achieved on a Broadway stage. The lighting for a small production might be achieved through a careful use of a few lightbulbs mounted on coffee cans and controlled by household wall switches. In either situation, an understanding of what the hardware is able to do and how it should be handled for safety and maximum effectiveness is essential.

There are many different types of lighting equipment used in the theater. However, they can be arranged into five main categories: lighting instruments, mounting equipment, electrical systems, control systems, and beam modification equipment. The following discussion deals mainly with lighting instruments and mounts—equipment you'll need to be familiar with to fulfill requirement 3g.

Lighting Instruments

Ellipsoidal reflector spotlights. Ellipsoidal reflector spotlights, variously known as lekos or klieg lights, have become the primary lighting instrument in the modern theater. These spotlights are used in virtually every location in the theater and for almost every possible purpose of stage lighting.

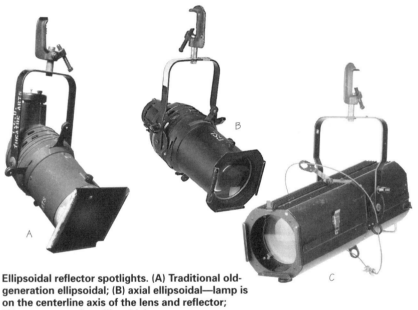

Ellipsoidal reflector spotlights. (A) Traditional old-generation ellipsoidal; (B) axial ellipsoidal—lamp is on the centerline axis of the lens and reflector; (C) new-generation ellipsoidal.

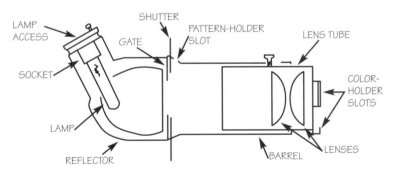

Ellipsoidal reflector spotlight

PAR can. A PAR can is one of the most practical theatrical lighting instruments available. A PAR can is a simple housing with a yoke, pipe clamp, color-holder slot, and socket. The heart of the instrument is the *parabolic aluminized reflector* or PAR lamp, which is mounted at the back of the housing with a spring ring to hold it in place. These lamps generally have a long life and are almost impossible to damage; they will withstand severe shock, and, when it is cool, it is completely safe to touch the glass portion of the lamp.

PAR can

Fresnel. A fresnel (pronounced fruh-nell) spotlight produces a soft-edged beam of concentrated illumination. This instrument is distinguished by its lens. If you look at it from the front, you see that the lens has a series of circles carved into it, but from the back, the flat surface is textured. This relatively thin piece of glass creates the effect of a very thick plano-convex lens.

Fresnel lens, side view

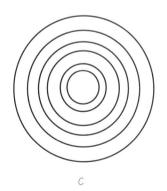

6" fresnel

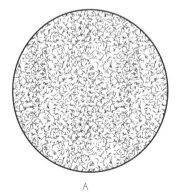

A   B   C

Fresnel lens: (A) back; (B) section; (C) front

Spotlights. Spotlights are intended to illuminate a specific area of the stage with a controlled beam of light. Spotlights use plano-convex lenses, which are flat on one side and curved outward on the opposite side.

Scoops. Also called ellipsoidal reflector floods (ERFs), scoops are the most common flood-lights in the modern theater.

Scoop with rotatable square color-holder slot

Border and strip lights. A long, narrow trough that contains several lights in a row is called a border light or strip light. The term "border lights" tends to refer to permanently installed continuous troughs that cross the entire stage. "Strip lights" are usually 6- to 8-foot-long sections of lights that are portable.

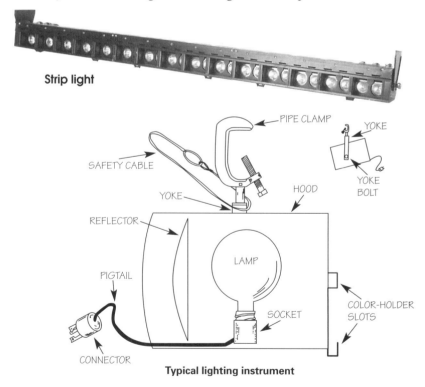

Strip light

Typical lighting instrument

Lighting Instrument Terms

Socket. The socket is a part of the fixture that holds the lamp (lightbulb) in place and conducts power to it. Although sockets are a fairly permanent part of most lighting instruments, they will wear out with age. Damaged sockets can be replaced.

Lamps. Lamps (lightbulbs) are designed to fit specific equipment based on the design of the socket, reflector, lens (when used), and the overall size of the lighting instrument.

Pigtail. The pigtail is the wire that comes out of the lighting instrument and ends in a plug.

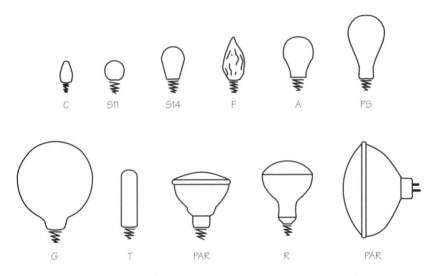

Lamp shapes: C is candelabra, S11 and S14 are spheres, F is flame, A is apple, PS is pear shape, G is globe, T is tube, PAR is projector and reflector, and R is reflector.

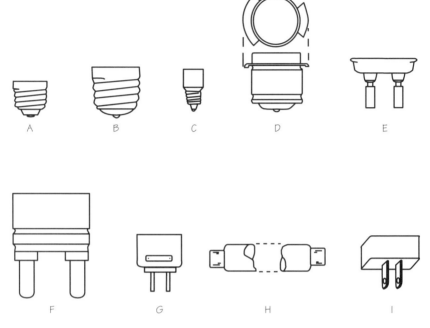

Lamp bases: (A) Medium screw base; (B) mogul screw base; (C) miniature screw base; (D) mogul prefocus; (E) medium bipost; (F) mogul bipost; (G) medium two pin; (H) double ended; (I) medium end pin.

Yoke. The yoke is a metal band that makes a loop around the lighting instrument and bolts to it on each side.

Pipe clamp. This clamp is attached to the yoke by a bolt. The pipe clamp is used to hang the lighting instrument from a pipe.

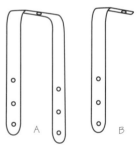

Mounting hardware: yoke (A), and hanger iron (B)

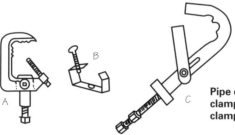

Pipe clamps: standard pipe clamp (A), lightweight pipe clamp (B), Sure-Grip clamp (C)

Safety chains and cables.
Safety chains and cables are used with all lights. A safety chain is an extra piece of lightweight cable or chain that is wrapped around the pipe from

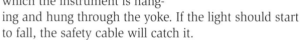

Safety cable

which the instrument is hanging and hung through the yoke. If the light should start to fall, the safety cable will catch it.

Caution: Whenever you are changing lamps on any fixture, always be sure that the circuit is turned off and the light is unplugged. Never touch the glass part of any bulb.

Many combinations of these and other stage lights will be used in a professional production to achieve beautiful results. Stage lighting is impossible to learn without practice. If possible, meet requirement 3g by actually handling the lighting for a play.

Electronic control board

Miming and Pantomiming

The word "mime" comes from the Greek word *mimos,* meaning "representation." Mime, then, is the art of acting out a message or a saying that is abstract. For example, one might act out the idea that a person drinks all the cola from a soft-drink bottle, then climbs into the bottle and becomes trapped.

Pantomime is similar to mime in that it is silent, but it retells a story, legend, or tale. Mime and pantomime both involve facial and body expressions in place of words. An everyday example is when the umpire crouches over a close play and spreads his arms wide with palms down. He is telling us that the runner is safe. In your classroom, when you raise your hand to answer a question, you are telling the teacher by pantomime that you know the answer—or at least you think you do.

Pantomime has a long and important place in the theater, going back to the earliest dramas. During some periods of the theater's history, pantomime almost *was* the theater because it was much more important than the words. Even today, for comedians like Billy Crystal and Robin Williams, pantomime is an important element in their performances.

Maybe you have had some practice in pantomime before now—in school or in a church presentation. Perhaps you were told to make up gestures and movements to suit the character you were playing. If so, it was excellent practice for requirement 4 because that is exactly what you are asked to do now.

To fulfill the requirement, you must be ready to pantomime any one of the five situations that your counselor asks for. Your counselor will not be satisfied with a very short, shoddy performance that you obviously have not prepared for. This means that you must think through each situation and then practice your movements and facial expressions so that they convey exactly what you want them to convey.

In the first situation, for example, when you enter the room, your counselor wants to see whether the room pleases you and you like what you find there. You might show by movement and expression that a picture on the wall is exquisite, that the furniture is dusty, and that the fruit in a bowl is rotting. Let your counselor experience through your pantomime the texture of the couch, the fragrance of roses in the vase, or the warmth of the room. Make up your own act and then practice it until you know that you can communicate an idea or emotion by pantomime.

Learning to Pantomime/Mime

Like any other actor, the mime must be a great observer of people. The mime must watch how they walk, the gestures they use when they talk, the way they look when they are sad. If you are going to create the illusion of reality through pantomime, you must know what the reality is. So closely watch other people before you try to imitate them in pantomime.

Of course, for this requirement you are asked only to play yourself, not an old man or a clown. But you will probably find it so much fun that you will want to do more of it. Then your observations of other people will be valuable.

Try to get a friend to practice pantomime with. You might think that all you have to do is practice before a mirror. This can be a help, but remember that pantomime is a performing art, so you really ought to have an audience to react to it. That's why it is best to practice with a friend.

The beginner mime must first learn some basic techniques before he can best portray his surroundings. One technique is the "wall" to show being confined in a room, a box, a bottle, etc. Be sure to know where your wall is! Begin with a fisted hand, then open it out and "press" on the wall. Now do the other hand. Be sure to watch your hands.

The wall

Now, with a flick of the wrist, remove one hand from the wall, loosely fist it, and replace it on the wall. Repeat.

A second technique is the "rope." You can be climbing up or pulling a rope. Imagine the "rope" about two or three inches in diameter. Hold it in both hands, one farther out than the other. Let go with the near hand, and make a flat hand. Keep the rope hand in the same place and lean with your torso. Replace your hand and (keeping the same distance between hands) pull the "rope" with your torso. Repeat.

Another technique is the "stick." As with the rope, hold your hands one about six inches above the other. Imagine the "stick" to be about two or three inches in diameter. Keep the hands the same distance apart. Pull the top hand down and the bottom hand up—reverse your right hand so that it is now on top of the stick. Move the stick vertically now, keeping your hands an equal distance apart.

Before you perform, observe people for a while. Note their facial, hand, and body expressions. Practice in front of a mirror, a video camera, or a friend. Remember body tension, facial expression, exaggeration, and the surroundings you have created. Don't walk into a "wall" or "table" you've already established.

Ideas for Skits

Besides the five situations described in requirement 4, you can work up other ideas for pantomime skits. You might have no trouble coming up with ideas, but remember that a pantomime skit should have a definite beginning, middle, and end. Also, it should have a conflict and resolution. Sixty to 90 seconds is a good length.

Some ideas for pantomime skits are:

- You're getting ready for school (include your routine) but you've lost your shoes.

- On a hike, you find a stick and throw it; it hits a beehive.

- *(For partners)* Bored, one partner has an idea. You play tug-of-war; one of you wins, the other sulks; then you make up.

- You're getting ready for bed (include your routine) but your sister or brother is in the bathroom.

You will find pantomime great fun even if you have no desire to become an actor. At the same time, you will be learning something about the actor's art.

Shoptalk at Theatre TCU

Talking Shop

The theater has an ancient tradition, and like any other business or profession it has developed its own jargon over the years. Many theater words—spotlight, for instance—are now used outside the theater. You might say, if you were called on in class, "I was put in the spotlight." In the theater, *spotlight* has the same general meaning but it also refers to a special kind of lighting instrument that does a special job.

A traditional greeting to an actor, given just before a performance, is "Break a leg." The saying is born of the superstition that if one wishes "Good luck," the perverse gods will send the opposite, but if one wishes misfortune, the gods will be tricked into sending an actor good luck.

There are thousands of technical words used among theatrical people, and there is no point in your trying to memorize a long list of them. But if you are going to work in the theater, you'll need to know a few simple terms. They can be learned quickly if you have a chance to work with a school drama or community theater group. Requirement 5 calls for you to explain, in your own words, the terms listed here.

Arena. An arena is a theater without a proscenium and usually without curtains. The spectators' seats rise gradually or in actual tiers, surrounding or nearly surrounding the stage. The stage itself may be a theater floor or a platform or platforms. This is called arena staging or central staging. It may also be called theater-in-the-round. Arena staging is especially good for a play with a small cast in which the action is confined to a small area. It is not so good for the bigger, spectacle-type of play in which there is a lot of physical action and movement on stage.

Batten. This is a horizontal pipe suspended from the flies, on which scenery and lights may be hung. A batten system consists of counterweighted battens on a pulley system that can be raised or lowered over the entire stage.

Center stage. Literally, this is the space at the very center of the acting area. It is also slang for being the focus of the audience's attention.

Flies. This is the area above the stage, hidden from the audience by a border or drapery, to which scenery can be lifted clear of the stage. It's also called the fly loft. Many modern theaters don't have such a space above the stage, and so are restricted to plays with a single set, minimal settings, or other conventional staging.

Floodlight. This is a light with a large reflector and a high-wattage lamp that produces a broad fill of light on the stage. Its beam is not easily controlled, but the light spreads illumination evenly.

Proscenium arch. This is the framing arch through which, in many theaters, the audience sees the play. Your school auditorium's stage probably has a proscenium arch.

Spotlight. This is a light that throws an intense beam on a defined area. Often when a spotlight is used, it is focused on a single actor and the rest of the stage is blacked out.

Stage brace. This is a rod hooked to the back of a flat at one end and weighted or screwed down to the floor at the other end. It is used to support a standing flat.

Stage crew. This is the backstage technical crew responsible for running the show. In small theater companies, often the same people build the set and handle the *load-in* (placing the set on the stage where the play is to be performed and anchoring it using such methods as bolting frames to the floor). Also, during performances, the stage crew changes the scenery and handles the curtain.

Stage right, stage left. These are areas on the stage as seen from the actor's perspective, as opposed to "house left and right," which are from the audience's perspective.

On Stage!

Requirement 6 is mostly just for fun. But that does not mean that you don't have to prepare for it or that you won't get anything out of it.

You probably enjoy singing or dancing or taking part in skits; if you did not, chances are you wouldn't even be trying to earn the Theater merit badge. So the requirement ought not to be too difficult to complete. You'll enjoy it more, though, and learn more about the theater, if you try to do some entertainment features that you have never done before.

Perhaps you sing well and have a good repertoire of songs. Fine; practice a song and use it to meet half of the requirement. But for your second act, how about trying a recitation or make up and perform a skit with a friend? In other words, don't take the easy way out. Try to learn some new act that could be given before your troop.

Prepare well. Your counselor will not be satisfied if it is clear that you have not practiced your act. When you go to your counselor, you should have the act polished so well that you would be glad to give it before an audience at that time.

What Next?

When you have earned the Theater merit badge, you will have mastered some of the fundamentals of work in drama. But you will still be a long way from Broadway or the professional stage anywhere.

In this pamphlet, we have not touched deeply on the difficulties and techniques of acting. We have barely scratched the surface of the director's art and of the complications in designing for the theater, and we have not considered at all such things as sound effects and special lighting. There are still great gaps in your knowledge.

You can learn about these things in special schools and workshops. If you intend to make the theater either your profession or your hobby, no doubt you will want to take these courses.

One excellent way to learn that does not involve formal study is to join a children's or community theater group. If there is not one in your community, there probably is one somewhere near. Search it out and offer your services. You may be given such unglamorous work as painting scenery, but that is not the whole story. You will also be learning something every time you appear at the theater. And you will be having fun and gaining experience at the same time.

Because of lack of space, we have not examined any of the great plays. They are well worth your time to study if you have an interest in the theater. Your school and public libraries as well as video stores will have shelves of the great plays.

We have not touched on such special branches of the theater as musical comedy and opera, or such things as variety acts, which are on the fringe of the theater world. All of these things will be of interest to you if your work on this merit badge has heightened your interest in the theater.

Now, as the curtain falls, one point worth repeating is: Get involved in the theater. Act in a Scout skit. Volunteer for play productions in your school. Join a theater group. Read and watch plays.

Scouting stresses learning by doing. So does the theater.

Theater Resources

Scouting Literature

Art, Cinematography, Communications, Journalism, Model Design and Building, Painting, and *Reading* merit badge pamphlets

Acting

Aitken, Maria, editor. *Style: Acting in High Comedy.* Applause, 1996.

Bruder, Melissa. *A Practical Handbook for the Actor.* Vintage Books, 1986.

Cole, Toby. *Acting: A Handbook of the Stanislavski Method.* Three Rivers Press, 1995.

Craig, David. *A Performer Prepares: A Guide to Song Preparation for Actors, Singers and Dancers.* Applause, 1996.

Daw, Kurt. *Acting: Thought into Action.* Heineman, 1997.

Hagen, Uta. *The Passion for Acting with Haskel Frankel.* Macmillan, 1973.

Jesse, Anita. *Let the Part Play You.* Third edition. Wolf Creek Press, 1994.

Kipnis, Claude. *The Mime Book.* Meriwether, 1994.

Silverberg, Larry. *The Sanford Meisner Approach: An Actors Workbook.* Smith and Kraus, 1994.

Theater Terms

Carter, Paul. *The Backstage Handbook: An Illustrated Almanac of Technical Information.* Third edition. Broadway Press, 1994.

Mobley, Jonnie Patricia, Ph.D. *NTC's Dictionary of Theatre and Drama Terms.* National Textbook Company, 1995.

History

Brown, John Russell, editor. *The Oxford Illustrated History of Theatre.* Oxford Press, 1997.

Esslin, Martin. *The Theatre of the Absurd.* Third edition. Penguin Books, 1991.

Henderson, Mary C. *Theatre in America.* Harry N. Abrams, 1996.

Playwriting

Catron, Louis E. *The Elements of Playwriting.* Macmillan, 1993.

Cohen, Edward M. *Playwright Working on a New Play.* Limelight Editions, 1995.

Korty, Carol. *Writing Your Own Plays: Creating, Adapting, Improvising.* Macmillan, 1986.

Directing

Clurman, Harold. *On Directing.* Simon & Schuster, 1997.

Converse, Terry John. *Directing for the Stage.* Meriwether, 1997.

Marowitz, Charles, Peter Brook, and Peter Brock. *Directing the Action.* Applause, 1996.

Stage Design

Aronson, Arnold. *American Set Design.* Theatre Communications Group, 1985.

James, Thurston. *The Prop Builder's Molding and Casting Handbook.* Betterway Books, 1989.

———. *The Theater Prop's Handbook.* Betterway Books, 1987.

Payne, Darwin Reid. *Scenographic Imagination.* Southern Illinois University Press, 1993.

Pecktal, Lynn. *Designing and Drawing for the Theatre.* McGraw-Hill, 1995.

Smith, Ronn. *American Set Design 2.* Theatre Communications Group, 1991.

Costume Design and Makeup

Barton, Lucy. *Historic Costume for the Stage.* Baker, 1967.

Bentley, Tony. *Costumes by Karinska.* Harry N. Abrams, 1995.

Braun and Schneider, Bertel Braun. *Historic Costumes in Pictures.* Dover, 1975.

Buchman, Herman. *Stage Makeup.* Billboard, 1979.

Corson, Richard. *Stage Makeup.* Sixth edition. Prentice-Hall, 1981.

Delamar, Penny. *The Complete Makeup Artist.* Northwestern University Press, 1996.

Ingham, Rosemary, Elizabeth Covey, and Liz Covey. *The Costume Designer's Handbook.* Prentice-Hall, 1986.

———. *The Costumer's Handbook.* Prentice-Hall, 1987.

Peacock, John. *Costume: 1066–1990s.* Thames & Hudson, 1994.

Lighting Design

Cunningham, Glen. *Stage Lighting Revealed: A Design and Execution Handbook.* Betterway Books, 1993.

Gillette, J. Michael. *Designing with Light: An Introduction to Stage Lighting.* Second edition. Mayfield, 1989.

Parker, W. Oren, Harvey K. Smith, and R. Craig Wolf. *Scene Design and Stage Lighting.* Sixth edition. Holt, Rinehart and Winston, 1990.

Walters, Graham. *Stage Lighting Step by Step.* Writer's Digest Books, 1997.

Plays for Youth

Cerf, Bennett, and Van H. Cartmell, editors. *Thirty Famous One-Act Plays.* Doubleday, 1963.

Lane, Eric, editor. *Telling Tales: New One-Act Plays.* Penguin, 1993.

Lane, Eric, and Nina Shengold, editors. *Take Ten: New 10-Minute Plays.* Vintage Books, 1997.

Slaight, Craig, and Jack Sharrar, editors. *Multicultural Scenes for Young Actors.* Smith & Kraus, 1991.

———. *Short Plays for Young Actors.* Smith & Kraus, 1996.

Smith, Marisa, editor. *The Seattle Children's Theatre: Six Plays for Young Actors.* Smith & Kraus, 1997.

Stein, Howard, and Glenn Young, editors. *The Best American Short Plays 1994–1995.* Applause, 1995.

———. *The Best American Short Plays 1995–1996.* Applause, 1997.

Acknowledgments

The Boy Scouts of America is grateful to the following organizations and individuals for assistance in preparing the 1999 edition of the *Theater* merit badge pamphlet:

Boy Scout Troop 508, Irving, Texas

Boy Scout Troop 1001, Richardson, Texas

Gemini Stage Lighting and Equipment Co. Inc., Dallas, Texas

Haltom High School Theatre Arts students of 1997–98 under supervision of Connie Sanchez, director, Haltom High School Theatre Arts program, Fort Worth, Texas

LaLonnie Lehman, Theatre TCU, Texas Christian University, Fort Worth, Texas

Lynne Moon, stylist

Kimberly G. Morris, costume designer and makeup artist (She provided the sketches used in the chapter "Designing Costumes.")

G. Joan Rambin, Stage West volunteer

Chris D. Shelton, drama major, Texas Woman's University, Denton, Texas

Stage West Theatre in Fort Worth, Texas; Diane Anglim, executive director

The BSA also thanks those who have contributed to previous editions of this pamphlet:

Century Lighting Company, Clifton, New Jersey

William Green, secretary-treasurer, American Society for Theatre Research

Harold I. Hansen, chairman, Dramatic Arts Department, Brigham Young University

John F. Hruby, drama director, Rider College Theater '59

H. Beresford Menagh, executive secretary-treasurer, American Educational Theatre Association

Allan Pierce, drama instructor, Rutgers Preparatory School

Elliot Taubenslag, director of children's theater groups, New York City, and drama coach, East Brunswick High School, New Jersey

Photography Credits

Byers, Daryl—pages 35, 39 (bottom), 48, 50, 62 (light A), 67, 72, 75

Daniels, Gene—pages 21, 76, 78

Grizzelle, Don—page 12

Haltom High School, Fort Worth, Texas—pages 12, 56, 57

Piland, Randy—page 13

Thanks also to Theatre TCU, Texas Christian University, Fort Worth, Texas, for the use of props shown in photos on pages 39 (front elevation, sight-line drawing), and 67 (electronic control board).

The BSA thanks the Addison Theatre Centre Mainstage for the use of the ground plan shown on page 39 (designed by Michael Robinson, drawn by Scott Guenther) and the lighting plot shown on page 60 (designed by David Natinsky).

Notes

Notes